MATT CHRISTOPHER

On the Court with...
Hakeem Olajuwon

D0835258

MATT CHRISTOPHER

On the Court with...
Hakeem Olajuwon

Little, Brown and Company

Boston   New York   Toronto   London

First Edition

Cover photograph by Barry Gossage

Library of Congress Cataloging-in-Publication Data

Christopher, Matt.
    On the court with — Hakeem Olajuwon / Matt Christopher. — 1st ed.
        p.   cm.
    Summary: Examines the life and career of the Houston Rockets'
star center who ranks in the NBA top ten for blocked shots, points
scored, and rebounding.
    ISBN 0-316-13721-9
    1. Olajuwon, Hakeem. — Juvenile literature.   2. Basketball
players — United States — Biography — Juvenile literature.
3. Houston Rockets (Basketball team) — Juvenile literature.
[1. Olajuwon, Hakeem.   2. Basketball players.   3. Houston Rockets
(Basketball team)   4. Nigerian Americans — Biography.]   I. Title.
GV884.O43C57   1997
796.323'092 — dc21
[B]   97-21551

10   9   8   7   6   5   4   3   2   1

COM-MO

Published simultaneously in Canada by Little, Brown & Company
(Canada) Limited

Printed in the United States of America

Contents

MATT CHRISTOPHER

On the Court with...
Hakeem Olajuwon

Chapter One:
1963-78

Beginning the Journey

The journey counts. When you get to the destination, you don't look back and say you should have done this or that. You enjoy it all the way through. Getting there is what really counts.

— Hakeem Olajuwon

Coming from Hakeem Olajuwon, star center of the Houston Rockets, those words ring true. For no other player in the National Basketball Association has made a journey quite like the one taken by Olajuwon. Olajuwon's love of basketball led him from Africa to the United States, first at the University of Houston and then with the Houston Rockets. His has been a journey filled with hard work, big dreams, and the constant desire to become a better player. It has made him a world champion, an Olympic gold medal winner, and one of the best players in the history of basketball.

1

Hakeem Olajuwon was born in Nigeria, a country in Africa. From watching movies and television, you may believe that Africa is covered by jungle and that animals like lions, hyenas, and elephants lurk around every corner.

In reality, only a small portion of the continent is jungle. In the north, Africa is dominated by the Sahara Desert. Large expanses of central and southern Africa are covered by the savanna, an area of grassland not unlike the Great Plains of the United States. Only the African interior, near the equator, is jungle. And as is true for most places in the world today, Africa's wild animals are quite rare and are confined to national parks or remote, little-populated areas.

Nigeria is located in West Africa, on what is referred to as the Guinea Coast. With more than 120 million citizens, it is the most populous country in Africa. It is also one of the larger nations on the continent, about the size of Texas. The south coast of Nigeria, along the Atlantic Ocean, is lush and humid, while the north is drier and part of the savanna.

Nigeria is one of the most modern African nations,

and the port city of Lagos, on the mouth of the Niger River, is an industrial and commercial center of more than a million people.

Hakeem Olajuwon was born in Lagos in 1963. His father, Salam, and mother, Abike, lived on the outskirts of the city. They were cement merchants, purchasing cement at the port and then selling it to builders. It was hard work, but the Olajuwons knew their business.

Hakeem was one of six children. He had an older half brother, Yemi Kaka; a sister, Kudirat; and three younger brothers — Akinola, Tajudeen, and Abdul Afis. The family belonged to the Yoruba tribe and spoke Yoruba at home. Their religion was Islam. Life was lived according to the culture of the Yoruba people and the traditions of the Islamic religion. While the children usually wore Western clothing, Hakeem's parents still dressed traditionally in long robes.

Salam and Abike kept a close eye on all their children, including Hakeem. They made sure they knew who his friends were. They did not allow him to spend time with anyone they did not approve of.

In the culture Hakeem grew up in, children who were troublemakers often found themselves shunned by their peers. If Hakeem or any of his friends started hanging around with the wrong crowd, others in the group would speak up. That made it easy to stay on the right track. A child who was well behaved, well mannered, hardworking, and intelligent was admired both by adults and by children.

Hakeem's parents were very strict but loving. All the children were expected to do their chores and treat their parents with respect. In return, the Olajuwons provided for their children and were always available to give them guidance.

Even though Nigeria was growing rapidly and the Olajuwons were well off, every young Nigerian dreamed of going to either Great Britain or the United States to study. At school, the Olajuwon children were expected to work hard and do well. Hakeem's older brother, Yemi, had set a fine example. He won a scholarship to study in Great Britain. The Olajuwons expected nothing less from Hakeem.

School in Nigeria is very demanding. So many different languages are spoken throughout the country that, beginning in the first grade, English is taught to all Nigerians so everyone will be able to communicate. In fact, most classes are taught in English. Students wear uniforms and have to pass difficult exams while adhering to high academic standards. There is little time for play.

Although Hakeem was an excellent student, particularly in math, there was nothing he liked better than playing. His home was in a complex of houses that surrounded a large open field. Whenever he could find the time after finishing his schoolwork and his household duties, Hakeem would race outside to play in the field with the other children.

Soccer was their favorite pastime. Sometimes they would play for hours as different players drifted in and out of the game.

Hakeem loved playing soccer. He had always been tall for his age and sometimes was teased by children at school. As a result, he was very shy. But when he played soccer, he forgot all about his height.

But Hakeem's parents thought that soccer was a waste of time. So when he was playing in the field, Hakeem always kept on the lookout for his parents' car. When he saw it coming down the road, he would race home, sit down at the table, open a book, and pretend that he was studying.

When Hakeem was twelve years old, his parents sent him to a boarding school called Aladura Comprehensive High School. He lived at the school and saw his parents only once a month, on visiting day.

It was difficult to be away from home, but one thing helped Hakeem adjust and make new friends. After class each day, the boys were allowed to play soccer!

He usually played goalkeeper. It was hard for the other teams to score on him. Whenever a player broke loose in front of the net and took a shot, there was Hakeem, stretching out his long arms and knocking the ball away. Other times he played fullback. Although the position is primarily a defensive one, every once in a while Hakeem would race downfield with the ball and try to score.

After one year at the boarding school, Hakeem transferred to Muslim Teachers College. Despite the name, the school was more like a high school than a college. After graduation, he could either teach if he chose to or go on to attend a university. He also received instruction in the Islamic religion. It was near his home, so he moved back and walked to school each day.

Best of all, the school sponsored its own sports teams that competed against other teachers schools. Although Hakeem was one of the younger students, he played goalkeeper on the soccer team and ran track. Everyone could tell that Hakeem was one of the best athletes at the school.

When Hakeem was fifteen, the school introduced a new sport — team handball. At first, Hakeem wasn't interested, but his friends couldn't stop talking about the new game. So Hakeem decided to give it a try.

Team handball is played by two teams of seven players and is something of a mixture of soccer and basketball. The ball is like a heavy volleyball, and the object of the game is to throw it into a goal about half the size of a soccer net. To move the ball downfield, players can dribble it like a basketball or pass it to another player.

Hakeem discovered that he was good at this new game. His hands were big, and he found it easy to grip the ball and throw it hard and fast into the net.

Hakeem particularly enjoyed setting up several yards in front of the goal with the ball. From there, he could shoot, fake a shot, or make a surprise pass to another player on his team. Within a few weeks, Hakeem felt as if he had been playing team handball his entire life. He was the best player on the team, and he stopped playing soccer to concentrate on the new game.

Each year, the Nigerian government sponsored a national athletic tournament for teachers schools, sort of like the Olympics. The Muslim Teachers College handball team was one of the best in Lagos, and Hakeem looked forward to competing against other schools in the country.

But just a few weeks before the sports festival, the team received some bad news. Because team handball was such a new sport, there were not enough teams to hold a tournament at the festival. The team handball competition was canceled.

Hakeem was devastated. He had looked forward to attending the tournament more than anything!

Then he had an idea. For months, the school's basketball coach, Ganiyu Otenigbade, had pleaded with Hakeem to give basketball a try. Hakeem was already six foot eight, and from watching him on the team handball court, Coach Ganiyu thought Hakeem might be a good player. "This is your game," he told him.

Hakeem had always refused. He had never played basketball; he didn't even understand the rules. But now, only a few weeks before the big festival, Hakeem changed his mind.

He decided to give basketball a try.

He approached Coach Ganiyu. As Olajuwon later described in his autobiography, *Living the Dream,* as soon as the coach saw him coming, he began to laugh. He knew how much Olajuwon wanted to go to the sports festival.

"Ah," he said when he saw the look on Hakeem's face, "I told you this was your sport."

All Hakeem said was "I want to play."

Suddenly Coach Ganiyu turned stern. As much as he wanted the tall fifteen-year-old on his team, he wanted to make sure that Hakeem was serious.

"Don't come here thinking you're just going to this tournament," he warned. "This is permanent."

Hakeem Olajuwon nodded his head in agreement. He was now a basketball player. But there was just one problem: Hakeem Olajuwon didn't have the faintest idea how to play. He had a lot to learn.

Chapter Two:
1978

The Big Man

Basketball was a mystery to Hakeem Olajuwon. Few Nigerians played, and there was no opportunity to view the sport on television. He had never even watched a full game. He had always been busy playing other sports.

Coach Ganiyu invited Hakeem to practice and led him onto the basketball court for the first time. At other outdoor courts the rest of the team practiced with some assistant coaches.

The head coach grabbed a basketball and told Hakeem to watch closely. Then he dribbled once, jumped, and made a layup, the easiest shot in basketball.

Olajuwon watched as the coach went up smoothly and shot the ball softly off the backboard and through the basket. This looks easy, he thought.

11

Then Coach Ganiyu handed the ball to Hakeem. "Now you try," said the coach.

The ball felt strange in his hands. It was bigger and lighter than the ball used in team handball. He tried to bounce the ball once then step toward the basket, jump, and lay the ball in the basket like his coach had.

He failed miserably. First, as he tried to control the ball after the dribble, he stumbled. Then he found himself too far away from the basket and jumped awkwardly. Finally, when the ball left his hands, it seemed as if it had a mind of its own and bounced harmlessly off the rim.

Hakeem was embarrassed, but the coach was patient. "Don't worry about making the shot," admonished Coach Ganiyu. "Just get the form, the technique."

Hakeem did as he was told. Within a few minutes, his body began to respond to the new commands he was giving it. His natural coordination, honed by years of playing soccer and team handball, took over. He started making layups!

Then the coach took the ball, jumped, and flipped in a short jump shot. Coach Ganiyu was a good player. When he was younger, he had played guard on the Nigerian national team. Not only did he coach at Hakeem's school but he coached at Lagos State University. He knew what he was doing on the basketball court. After demonstrating the jump shot a few more times, he handed the ball back to Olajuwon and asked him to try.

Hakeem tried to remember how the coach had held the ball, raising it above his head as he jumped, and how at the peak of his jump he had effortlessly flicked the ball through the basket.

Once more Hakeem held the strange ball in his hands. He jumped and at the top of his leap tried to release the ball and steer it toward the basket. It fell short. Hakeem Olajuwon had shot an air ball!

Once again the coach told him not to worry, to concentrate on his form. "Don't push the ball," he said. "Shoot it with your wrist."

Hakeem tried again. Each time, he got a little better. Within a few minutes, he started sinking the jumper — not every time, but often enough to make him feel that he was making progress.

The coach asked his assistant to run the practice with the rest of the team. For the next two hours, Coach Ganiyu worked only with Hakeem.

The coach was impressed. Hakeem was more than just tall. He was coordinated and moved gracefully. He was also intelligent and eager to learn. After only two hours, Hakeem Olajuwon was already more skilled than some members of the team who had been playing basketball for several years. As Olajuwon later recalled in his autobiography, over and over Coach Ganiyu told him, "This is your sport, it's a big man's game. You are the kind of person we need in basketball."

Then he said something that really got Hakeem's attention. "This game," he said, "is played in America."

When Hakeem heard the coach mention America, his eyes grew wide. America, he thought, that's where I want to go someday.

Then Olajuwon really began to learn the game. The coach taught him what a rebound was and how to get one. He explained the three-second rule (a player can't remain in the free throw lane for more than three seconds). He showed Hakeem how to throw a chest pass and how to block a shot.

"This is big man's territory," said Coach Ganiyu

while standing under the basket. "You have to play like a big man!"

Hakeem soaked up every word. After a while, the coach asked the team's point guard to join them so Hakeem could learn to pass the ball to start a fast break. Then Hakeem watched the remainder of the practice, so he could see the fundamentals he had just been taught put to use.

Now basketball began to make sense to Hakeem. He saw the team's center fight for rebounds, then throw the ball quickly to a guard to start the fast break. He watched the center set up down low, catch a pass, then spin in for a layup. Hakeem started falling in love with basketball.

After practice ended, Coach Ganiyu spoke privately with Hakeem. "You have tremendous potential," he told him. "A player like you doesn't come around very often."

Two days later, Hakeem traveled to the sports festival as a member of the basketball team.

In its first game, the team played Kano, the pretournament favorite. Kano's best player was its center. Although he stood only six foot five, everyone called him Big Man. None of the players knew his real name.

Olajuwon watched Big Man closely. Big Man could already do all the things Coach Ganiyu had tried to teach Hakeem. He played big, intimidating other players so much that no one would challenge him under the basket. Hakeem's team fell behind almost immediately.

Then Coach Ganiyu yelled for Hakeem. He was going into the game!

Big Man looked at Hakeem strangely. He had never played against anyone who was bigger than he was. He wondered if this new player knew what he was doing.

For the next few minutes, Hakeem got a fast lesson in basketball. Big Man used his experience and strength to completely befuddle Olajuwon. On offense, he pushed Hakeem around under the basket to get position. When he got the ball, all he had to do was fake a shot to send Hakeem soaring into the air. Then Big Man either dribbled by him for an easy basket or allowed Hakeem to land on him for an obvious foul.

Hakeem did a little better when his team had the

ball. Although Big Man still pushed Hakeem around and got position under the basket, Olajuwon used his height to collect his share of rebounds. Still, Muslim Teachers College lost badly. But for the rest of the tournament, Hakeem watched the game closely, particularly Big Man. He knew he still had a long way to go.

After the tournament, Coach Ganiyu put Hakeem on the team at Lagos State. Although everyone else on the team was much older and more experienced, the coach knew that for Hakeem to improve, he had to practice against better competition.

For a while, Hakeem continued to play team handball, too, but he soon quit the game. Basketball became the focus of his life. The more he played, the better he became.

Hakeem learned that he could block shots made by smaller players. He loved pinning the ball against the backboard or letting a player drive past him, then reaching out to swat the ball away from behind. He discovered how to use his size to block out other players and grab rebounds. He stopped leaping after every fake and held his position. In just a few short weeks, he became a very good defensive player.

Playing offense was more difficult. Hakeem struggled. He found it hard to grow accustomed to holding the ball. He just didn't feel comfortable trying to jump and shoot at the same time.

Then one day at practice, as the coach was talking to the team, Olajuwon idly dribbled once, jumped, and without even thinking, dunked the ball through the basket. His teammates looked at him in awe.

Only one other member of the team could dunk, and he had to start running at half-court to do so.

Even Coach Ganiyu was impressed. "Do that again," he ordered. Once more Hakeem jumped and stuffed the ball through the hoop.

Each time he did so, a great wide smile broke out on Hakeem's face. Dunking was fun!

Now he posed a threat on offense. He was becoming a complete player.

Three months later, the Lagos State team traveled to the National Sports Festival. They faced Kano in their first game.

Hakeem would have to play Big Man!

For the first few minutes of the game, it appeared that Kano would win big. Each time one of the Lagos State players drove toward the basket, there was Big

Man, blocking the path and swatting the ball away. Kano made several fast-break baskets and took an early lead.

Then something happened. Big Man got the ball down low. Without hesitating, he went to the basket. *Swat!* Hakeem easily reached out and batted the ball away.

The crowd grew quiet, and people whispered back and forth, pointing at Hakeem. No one had ever blocked a shot by Big Man before!

Hakeem grew more confident. He suddenly realized that he was a better player than Big Man. Then he became the intimidator.

The game was close and went down to the last few seconds, but Lagos State held on to win. Hakeem Olajuwon had completely shut down Big Man.

The win was reported in all the newspapers in Lagos. Hakeem's parents couldn't believe it. All of a sudden, their son was famous. Hakeem's mother even started a scrapbook to hold all the clippings.

With that well-publicized victory, basketball became an even greater part of Hakeem's life. At school, he was allowed to go off-campus to the National Sports Stadium. Almost every day he played pickup basketball with his Lagos State teammates.

They played just as pickup basketball is played on American playgrounds. The winning team stays on the court until it is defeated. Sometimes Hakeem played four or five hours at a stretch. Each day, he got better and better.

One afternoon he noticed a man even taller than he was standing off to the side, watching closely. When the game finally broke up, the man approached Olajuwon and introduced himself. He was an American named Richard Mills, who worked for the Nigerian National Sports Commission, the government agency that sponsored Nigeria's national and Olympic teams. He asked Hakeem how long he had been playing basketball. Hakeem told him only a few months.

The man looked at Hakeem with surprise. "You play very well," he told him. "Could I give you a drive back to your home?"

Hakeem readily accepted. He was thrilled that someone from the National Sports Commission, particularly someone from *America,* thought he was a good player.

When they arrived at the Olajuwon house, Mills,

who also went by the Nigerian name Olawale, asked to meet Hakeem's parents.

He greeted them respectfully and then began talking. "Your son is unique," he told them. "Have you ever seen him play basketball?"

Hakeem's parents shook their heads.

Olawale chose his words carefully. "He will be a great player," he said slowly. "One day he will go to America for college, and play."

When Olawale said the words *America* and *college*, Hakeem's jaw dropped open. His parents were stunned. They looked at each other in wonder.

They knew that Hakeem was a very good player, but they had no idea that basketball might get their son into an American college.

As he was leaving, Olawale asked Hakeem to report to the stadium the following day to practice with the national team.

They could always use a big man.

Chapter Three:
1979–80

The National Team

Since he first had begun playing basketball, Hakeem Olajuwon tried to learn as much about the game as he could. In Nigeria, the very best players were on the national team. Over the past several months, Hakeem had heard stories about the national team but had never seen it play. Now he was going to play with the team!

For the first time in his life, he was also playing on an indoor court with a wooden floor. So far, he had played only outdoors, on cement or blacktop.

Olawale introduced Hakeem to all the players on the national team. One man stood out.

His name was Yommy Sangodeyi, but everyone called him Yommy Basket because it seemed that every time he shot the ball, he scored. Yommy was six foot ten — taller than Hakeem, older, and much more skilled. Since the first day he had played basketball, Hakeem had heard people speak of Yommy Basket.

When the practice began, Olajuwon could hardly believe the national team was playing the same game. Everyone moved so quickly and was so strong! Most of the players were ten or fifteen years older than he was and much more experienced. Hakeem felt as if he were playing the game for the first time.

Even so, Olawale and the other coach, another American named Oliver Johnson, were impressed by the young man's ability. They placed him on both the national team and the junior team, which represented Nigeria but was made up of younger players.

Although Hakeem practiced with the team nearly every day, he still had to attend school and his parents still expected him to do well academically. Suddenly, his days were very long. He woke up before the sun to do his schoolwork, was in class all day, and then spent several hours at basketball practice. Before going to bed at night, he still had more homework to do. Until the school year ended, Hakeem had never been so busy in all his life.

During school vacation that summer, Hakeem joined the national team full-time. The team spent several weeks living in a hotel and holding training camp in preparation for a big international tournament.

The players worked hard. Each morning, they ran three miles, then lifted weights. After that, they practiced for several hours. Hakeem couldn't believe how much his life had changed!

Hakeem tried to learn as much as possible from Yommy Basket. Yommy didn't mind helping him out. He knew that Hakeem Olajuwon had potential.

Hakeem traveled with the team to France and Morocco for tournaments. He was amazed to learn that there were so many good basketball players!

Almost every team had several players even taller than Yommy Basket. Hakeem wasn't sure he would ever be able to play well enough to help the team.

But on a few occasions when Yommy Basket got into foul trouble, Hakeem got to play. He surprised himself. Although he didn't dominate play, he made a good enough showing to impress his coaches.

When he returned to Nigeria, he rejoined the junior team. It was preparing to play in a big tournament against other African junior teams in Angola, a large country south of Nigeria on Africa's west coast.

After practicing with the national team, Hakeem Olajuwon was much better than most junior players. He had turned sixteen and now stood six foot ten, although he was still skinny and weighed less than 200 pounds.

Hakeem dominated most of Nigeria's opponents. Players all across Africa began hearing about the young center from Nigeria. In one game against Togo, a very small country west of Nigeria, Hakeem scored 60 points!

Still, Nigeria lost in the tournament semifinals to Central Africa, which had a center nearly as good as Hakeem. The two men neutralized each other. Central Africa played smart, disciplined basketball and won a close contest. It finished second in the tournament to Angola.

After the tournament, Hakeem was relaxing in his hotel room when a messenger knocked on the door and told him a white man wanted to talk with him. Hakeem ignored the messenger. He didn't know any white men and thought the messenger had made a mistake.

A few minutes later, the messenger came back with a note from the white man. His name was Christopher Pond, the coach of Central Africa, and he wanted to talk with Hakeem.

Curious, Hakeem met the man in the hotel restaurant. Pond peppered Olajuwon with questions.

"Is it true that you just started playing seven months ago?" he asked. Hakeem told him it was. Then he asked if Hakeem planned to go to a university. Hakeem told him that he did. His senior year of school was nearly complete, and soon he would have to decide where to go.

Pond paused. "Don't go to college in Nigeria," he said. "Go to the United States. If I can arrange for a scholarship and a visa, would your parents buy you a plane ticket?"

Hakeem Olajuwon could not believe his ears. A scholarship to an American college would be a dream come true. And a visa, a document granting official permission from the American government to enter the country, was almost impossible to get. Yet this man made it sound like the easiest thing in the world!

The next day, Pond took Hakeem to the American embassy in Angola. They met with the American ambassador, and Pond started calling his contacts at several American colleges. "I have a player who would be an All-American," he told them. Several schools agreed to take a look at Hakeem Olajuwon if he could get to America.

The American ambassador called his counterpart at the American embassy in Nigeria and explained the situation. The Nigerian ambassador agreed to meet with Olajuwon and Pond in several weeks when Hakeem had returned to Nigeria and the Central African team was scheduled to be in Lagos.

When Hakeem returned home, his head was swimming. He was so excited, he could hardly sleep. But he was also worried. For him to get to America, his parents had to be able to buy a round-trip plane ticket to the United States. That would cost thousands of dollars.

When he met his parents, he was surprised when his father pulled out the scrapbook that included clippings from the tournament in Angola. He was obviously very proud of his son. Still, Hakeem was afraid to ask for the money for the ticket. He asked his mother first; then she explained the situation to his father.

The Olajuwons were skeptical. While Hakeem had been in Angola, several Nigerian universities had offered him a scholarship. And Hakeem's parents worried that if an American college didn't offer him a scholarship, the money for the plane ticket would be lost forever. They were already paying for Hakeem's sister to attend the American University in Cairo, Egypt, and didn't have much money to spare.

Hakeem's parents told him that they wanted to speak with Mr. Pond before making a decision.

The next few weeks crept by as Hakeem waited for Pond to arrive. When he finally did, Hakeem went to see him. They immediately traveled to the American embassy.

A long line snaked outside the compound. Hundreds of Nigerians were hoping to get a visa.

Hakeem and Pond went to the front of the line and were swept inside. They sat with the American ambassador while Pond explained the situation.

Since first meeting Hakeem Olajuwon, Pond had arranged for visits to five American colleges — St. John's University, in New York; Providence College, in Rhode Island; North Carolina State; the University of Georgia; and the University of Houston, in Texas.

The ambassador was impressed. He told Hakeem to come back with his plane ticket and his passport, and he would give him a visa.

Hakeem's feet barely touched the ground as he raced home. But his heart was in his throat. He had to ask his parents for the plane ticket. Without the ticket, all the talk about going to America would be just that — talk.

As soon as he returned home, he told his parents about the meeting. His father was still skeptical. A round-trip ticket to America cost nearly five thousand dollars. His father said the family just couldn't take a chance with that kind of money.

Hakeem was crushed. Then his mother led Hakeem from the room. "I will speak to your father some more," she told him.

That night, Hakeem could not sleep. He sat in the living room wide awake, his heart pounding.

In the middle of the night, his mother awoke and found him sitting in the dark.

"Hakeem," she said softly. "I will talk with your

father. If he says no, I will give you the money my-self. Now go to bed."

He went right to sleep.

The next day, his parents gave him the money. Hakeem purchased the ticket and went right to the embassy. Within a few minutes, he received his visa.

When he returned home, he showed his parents the precious document. His mother started crying. "This is from Allah, this is from God," she said.

His father looked at the visa and nodded his head in agreement. "It is God's will," he told Hakeem.

Never before had his father looked at him with such pride. Hakeem was happy and sad at the same time. Happy to be going to America, but sad because he now realized he would have to leave his parents, the two people in the world he loved most. He promised himself that he would make his parents proud and never let them down.

In ten days, he would travel to America.

Chapter Four:
1980–81

Coming to America

When Hakeem Olajuwon first told his friends that he was going to America, they thought he was joking and didn't believe him. Then, when they realized he was serious, some of them became jealous. Hakeem knew the trip would change his life.

One of the first people he told of his good fortune was Yommy Basket. Yommy looked him in the eye and said, "Fight hard. Let them know there are basketball players in Africa." He knew that if Hakeem succeeded, it would open the door for other African players to go to college in America.

Hakeem nodded. Everyone was depending on him. He would do his best not to let them down.

The next ten days went by in a blur. Before he knew it, he was on a plane flying to New York.

He was scheduled to visit St. John's University first.

When he got off the plane in New York, he collected his bags and stepped outside the terminal.

As soon as he set foot on the sidewalk, Hakeem was hit in the face by a cold gust of wind. It was mid-October, and autumn was in the air.

Hakeem had never before felt such cold. He stepped back into the airport and looked at his ticket. His next stop was supposed to be Houston. He had been told it was warm in Houston.

He went to the ticket counter and showed the agent his ticket. "I want to go to Houston," he said.

The agent took his ticket with a puzzled look on her face. "But sir, you're not supposed to go to Houston for two more days."

"I want to go now," said Hakeem. He had had enough of the cold weather.

The agent changed the ticket. Four hours later, Hakeem Olajuwon left for Houston.

When he stepped outside in Houston, he felt better. It was much warmer than New York City. He got a taxi and went straight to the basketball office at the University of Houston. An assistant coach greeted him and started showing him around. The team was holding an informal practice, and the assistant asked

Hakeem if he wanted to play. When Hakeem nodded yes, the coach instructed the equipment manager to get Olajuwon a uniform and new shoes.

Hakeem could hardly believe his ears. New shoes? In Nigeria, new basketball shoes were as rare as diamonds. In fact, basketball shoes in any condition or of any size were hard to find. Ever since Hakeem had started playing basketball, he had played in an old pair of size thirteen tennis shoes, the largest size he was able to find. Even so, he had to curl up his toes to fit into them. They had always hurt his feet, but he had no other choice.

The manager looked at Hakeem's feet and asked what size he wore. Hakeem said, "Thirteen." The manager laughed. He went into a room and came out with several boxes of shoes.

He first had Hakeem try on a pair of size fourteen shoes. "Too tight," said the manager. Then Hakeem tried on a pair of size fifteen. They were still too tight.

Hakeem's mouth hung open as the manager pulled out a brand new pair of size sixteen basketball shoes. They fit him perfectly! For the first time since he had started playing basketball, Hakeem Olajuwon had a pair of shoes that didn't make his feet hurt. When he got on the court, he couldn't stop jumping!

He played in a pickup game with the other University of Houston players. Over and over again, when they would drive down the lane to shoot, Hakeem would jump up and swat the ball away. The players were impressed. So was the assistant coach.

He arranged for Olajuwon to meet head coach Guy Lewis the following morning. When he did, Coach Lewis offered Hakeem a scholarship.

Hakeem readily agreed. But the coach was worried about one thing. In order to qualify for the scholarship, Hakeem would have to obtain his GED, or general equivalency diploma, which is similar to a high school diploma. Although he had graduated from Muslim Teachers College, that degree wasn't recognized in the United States.

Coach Lewis took Hakeem to the admissions office and arranged for him to study with a tutor. He warned him that the test was very hard and that he would have to study for days, maybe even weeks, until he passed.

Now Hakeem was worried. The test sounded very difficult.

Then he met with his tutor. She handed him a pile of books and told him he would have to study them.

Hakeem picked up the books and started flipping through the pages. Then he started laughing.

His studies in Nigeria had been much more challenging. He had covered the material in the books years before. He asked to take the test immediately, and he passed without any problem. Hakeem Olajuwon was now an official student of the University of Houston.

Basketball season was just about to begin. The Houston coaches decided that it would be awkward for Hakeem to join the team so soon before the season. They decided to have him practice with the team and learn the plays. He would not play until the following season.

That was fine with Hakeem Olajuwon. There was a lot to get used to in America, and he knew he would need some time.

Everything in America was different. In Nigeria, almost every meal included rice. But in the school cafeteria at Houston, there was steak and chicken almost every day. Hakeem couldn't believe it.

And there was ice cream! Hakeem got a small refrigerator in his room and started taking back little cups of ice cream from the cafeteria so he could eat some whenever he liked. In his first year at Houston, he gained almost fifty pounds!

There were other adjustments to make, too. Hakeem spoke very formal English but wanted to learn to speak and to understand the slang used by his teammates. He also behaved very formally, bowing to people when he first met them. It took him a while to learn American customs.

But there was one part of American life he found easy to learn — basketball! He practiced with his teammates nearly every day and then went to a local park to play more basketball. He also watched as much of the game as possible on television. He was mesmerized by the skills of NBA stars like Julius "Doctor J" Erving, David Thompson, and Moses Malone.

But all the while he was learning about America, Hakeem did not forget where he came from. His coaches asked him whether there were other good players in Africa, and Hakeem told them about Yommy Basket. Within a few weeks, Yommy was in America, too, attending Sam Houston State University, just outside Houston. Hakeem had kept his promise to his friend.

The school year passed quickly. Although Olajuwon's coaches worried that he might have trouble with his courses and wanted him to take easy classes, he chose a rigorous schedule and passed easily. In Nigeria, he had developed discipline and good study habits, so despite playing basketball every day, he still knew how to get his schoolwork done and keep up with his studies.

The following summer, Hakeem was invited to play basketball at Houston's Fonde Recreation Center. At Fonde, the best players in the city played pickup games. Often, even professional players showed up to play.

Hakeem was honored to be invited. The great Moses Malone, star center for the Houston Rockets, was a regular at the rec center. Hakeem would have an opportunity to learn from one of the best players in the game.

In the 1980–81 season, Malone had led the Rockets to the NBA finals, where they had lost to Boston in six games. He played a tough, physical game; had a variety of moves underneath the basket; and was the best rebounder and one of the strongest players in the game. He didn't take it easy on Hakeem.

Malone continually challenged Olajuwon, forcing him to use his size and strength. At first, Hakeem was almost helpless against Malone, who seemingly scored at will and grabbed every rebound. When Olajuwon got the ball, Malone hounded him mercilessly, blocking his shots or forcing him to shoot off balance.

But by playing against Malone each day, Hakeem improved rapidly. Within a few weeks, he wasn't getting embarrassed anymore.

Malone was impressed. He befriended Hakeem, giving him clothes and pocket money. Hakeem was very grateful. He thought of Moses Malone as an older brother.

Before too long, local sportswriters began to hear stories about the young man from Africa who was playing so well against Moses Malone at Fonde. They were intrigued and investigated for themselves. The African, they wrote, was going to be a star.

Chapter Five:
1981–82

Final Four

When Hakeem Olajuwon joined the University of Houston varsity team in the fall of 1981, the Houston Cougars were already one of the best teams in college basketball. Guard Rob Williams was an All-American, while youthful forwards Clyde Drexler and Michael Young showed great promise.

Coach Guy Lewis was one of the most experienced coaches in the country. A number of former University of Houston players, like center Elvin Hayes and guard Don Chaney, had become stars in the NBA. Yet the Cougars had never won an NCAA championship — they hadn't even won an NCAA tournament game in ten years. The previous year, Houston had lost in the first round to Villanova.

The 1981–82 Cougars had the potential to be one of the best Houston teams in years. Some people were even predicting that the Cougars would reach the NCAA Final Four in the year-end tournament. The reason was Hakeem Olajuwon.

The Cougars liked to fast-break and play pressure defense. But in order to do so effectively, they needed a big man in the middle who could keep the other team from penetrating and who could rebound, get the ball out quickly, and then run the floor. That player was Hakeem.

At practice each day, the team worked on the fast break over and over again. Olajuwon loved grabbing a rebound, flicking an outlet pass to one of his guards, and then racing down the court. Watching him, it was hard to believe he had been playing basketball for only a year and a half.

Coach Lewis told Hakeem that his primary responsibility was to rebound and play tough defense. On offense, he was the team's last option. The other players, like Williams, Drexler, and Young, were supposed to take most of the shots. Olajuwon got the ball and scored only on follow-ups after the other players missed.

Hakeem worked hard in practice and made the starting lineup. Then, just when the official season was about to start, he hurt his back. He barely played in the team's first two games. He finally had to sit out several games entirely. By the time he recovered, people had almost forgotten about him.

When he returned, he started back slowly, playing only late in the game, when Houston was already way ahead. But it didn't take long for Hakeem to start receiving significant playing time. Although he didn't always start, he was one of the first players off the bench.

Fans soon looked forward to his playing. When Hakeem entered the game, they knew they would soon start seeing some blocked shots and fast breaks.

At first, many fans had a hard time pronouncing Hakeem Olajuwon's name, particularly *Olajuwon*. Then a sportswriter started referring to him as "the Dream," because his sudden appearance at the University of Houston had been so fortuitous. Fans started calling him "the Dream," too. The nickname has stuck with him through the years.

The Cougars blew hot and cold all year long. They would run off a big winning streak and crack the top twenty in the national polls, then drop several close games. Although they finished second in their league, the Southwest Conference, the Cougars ended the regular season unranked.

Nevertheless, they still received an invitation to the NCAA tournament. But no one expected them to do very well. Everyone believed that like the previous year's team, the Cougars would lose their first game.

Before the game, Coach Lewis challenged his players. "In two weeks I'm going to the Final Four," he told them. "It would be great if you guys could come with me."

The Cougars understood. Coach Lewis was telling them that he thought they were good enough to make the tournament finals.

At the time, only forty-eight teams were in the NCAA tournament. To reach the semifinals, or the Final Four, the Cougars would have to win four games.

In the regional semifinals, Houston played the Missouri Tigers, ranked number five in the country. Paced by their big All-American center Steve Stipanovich, Missouri was a big favorite. The Tigers dreamed of going to the Final Four themselves.

But *the* Dream, Hakeem Olajuwon, helped turn

Missouri's dream into a nightmare. Even though he was in only his second year of basketball, Hakeem played Stipanovich tough. The Cougars outhustled the favored Tigers, and Houston won by one point in a big upset.

The win gave the young team confidence. Two victories later, they made the Final Four!

The team traveled to New Orleans for the Final Four. The games were scheduled to be played in the Superdome, a stadium that seats more than 60,000 people.

Louisville, North Carolina, and Georgetown were the other three teams. The two semifinal games were scheduled to be played on a Saturday. The winners would then meet on Monday for the championship.

The Cougars played North Carolina. The Tar Heels were favored heavily.

They were also very talented. Forward James Worthy and center Sam Perkins were both All-Americans. Freshman guard Michael Jordan was just beginning to make his mark. All three went on to spectacular professional careers.

In the first half of the game, the Cougars played North Carolina even, but in the second half the Tar

Heels began to pull away. For the first time all season, Houston's opponent was even quicker than the Cougars were. North Carolina won, 68–63. Two days later, Hakeem watched on television from his hotel room as North Carolina beat Georgetown by one point in the finals to become the national champions.

Hakeem Olajuwon's journey had taken him all the way to the Final Four but left him short of his goal. He wanted another chance.

Chapter Six:
1982-84

Phi Slama Jama

Hakeem Olajuwon was becoming more accustomed to life in the United States. After the season ended, he moved off-campus and learned to drive. In the summer, he got a job working for an oil company. His major was in business administration, and the work experience would help him in a career after graduation.

Yet there were some aspects of American life he just couldn't get used to. When Olajuwon went out to nightclubs with some of his friends and teammates, he couldn't believe how they behaved. As a Muslim, Hakeem wasn't supposed to drink alcohol, but he didn't take his religion very seriously and occasionally drank a beer. Still, he was amazed to see how much many young Americans drank! He often became embarrassed as he watched their behavior get out of control.

He also found it hard to believe how his friends treated women. They spoke rudely to them and treated them with little respect. In Nigeria, Hakeem had been taught to be polite and always treat a woman with respect. While he adopted many of the ways of his new country, Hakeem Olajuwon's personality never changed. He remained polite and respectful of other people.

Despite his growing fame as a basketball player, Hakeem was very shy. He hunched over when he walked and tried to look shorter. He also avoided large crowds where he might be recognized. He was most happy when he was playing basketball, studying, or relaxing at home.

When he wasn't working for the oil company, he spent much of the following summer at Fonde, playing basketball with Moses Malone and other talented players in the Houston area. Olajuwon's game kept improving. Now he had the skills to occasionally put the ball on the floor and drive around Malone to the basket. The student was quickly catching up with the teacher.

Based upon their performance in the NCAA tournament the year before, the 1982–83 Cougars were expected to make the Final Four again. Anything less than a national championship would be a disappointment.

Team practices were intense and hard-fought. Most of the Houston players were great leapers, and there was nothing they enjoyed more than jamming the ball on one another.

Unlike some coaches, Guy Lewis didn't mind it when his team slam-dunked the basketball. He knew that opportunities to dunk usually stemmed from good defense and fast breaks, when his team was running the floor. If that was the case, it was all right with him if they finished the play with a jam. After all, reasoned the coach, the game was supposed to be fun.

In the first few games of the season, the Cougars won by huge margins. It seemed as if every time they ran down the floor, someone dunked the basketball. Fans were thrilled by the team's exciting play.

A clever sportswriter decided that the team needed a nickname. The one he chose spoofed the name of fraternities, like the Phi Beta Kappa. Since all the Cougars did was slam and jam, he figured their "fraternity" name should reflect that. He dubbed them Phi Slama Jama.

The players loved the name and the notoriety that came with it. Sportswriters all across the country picked up on it, and the Cougars became the best-known collegiate team in America.

After losing close games to Syracuse and Virginia, two of the best teams in college basketball, the Cougars went on a long winning streak. Olajuwon just kept improving.

He led the nation in blocked shots and was slowly becoming an ever more important part of the Cougars' offense. The opposition couldn't afford to forget about him for a second. If Hakeem's man left him to double-team Clyde Drexler or any other Cougar player, Hakeem was usually wide open. When he got the ball then, it was an automatic jam!

The Cougars successfully swept through the regular season. Then, in the conference tournament, they easily defeated their archrival, Arkansas, even though the Razorbacks' roster included four players — Darrell Walker, Alvin Robertson, Scott Hastings, and Joe Kleine — who would later go on to have productive professional careers. On many occasions, the Cougars' practice games against one another were closer contests than the real games.

Once the NCAA tournament began, the Cougars didn't slow down. They cruised past Maryland, Memphis State, and Villanova to reach the Final Four for the second year in a row. This time, the finals were played in Albuquerque, New Mexico.

In the semifinals, the Cougars were matched against the Louisville Cardinals. In every poll, Houston and Louisville were rated either the number one or number two team in the country. Many observers considered the semifinal matchup the true championship game and were referring to it as "the game of the century."

The Cardinals were the only team that ran and dunked like the Cougars. In fact, the Cardinals even had their own nickname — the Doctors of Dunk.

The game was played at a breakneck pace. Both teams raced up and down the court, dunking the ball on nearly every possession.

After trailing by five at halftime, the Cougars dug in during the second half. Olajuwon was a blocking machine. Time after time, Louisville players charged toward the basket, only to find Hakeem blocking their path. If they tried to shoot over him, he blocked their shots. Even when he didn't get a block, he often forced them to change their shots and shoot awkwardly. Then Hakeem would pull down the rebound and fire an outlet pass to start the fast break.

With five minutes left to play, the Cougars led by nine. Three plays by Hakeem Olajuwon put the game out of Louisville's reach.

On the first play, Cougar guard Alvin Franklin started to penetrate, then saw Hakeem break free under the basket. He fired a sharp pass that Olajuwon took on the run and threw through the hoop for a thunderous jam. The next time down the court, teammate Michael Young threaded a pass to Hakeem, who threw down a slam dunk with even more authority than the first one. Then, the next time down the court, they did it again.

On three straight possessions, Hakeem had finished the play with a spectacular slam. His outburst was met with tremendous applause. The Cougars went on to win, 94–81. He finished with 21 points, 22 rebounds, and 8 blocks — more than any other player on the court. The Cougars were going to the finals!

In the other semifinal game, North Carolina State upset Georgia. The Wolfpack had lost ten games in the regular season, and everyone considered their appearance in the finals a fluke. No one gave them a chance against Hakeem and Houston.

But in the finals, NC State played a tough, smart game. They weren't nearly as fast and talented as the Cougars, but they were bigger and shot better from outside. They slowed down the game and controlled the tempo.

Still, late in the second half, the Cougars finally got their running game going. Just as he had in the semifinal, Hakeem Olajuwon scored on a couple of monster dunks. With only three minutes left, Houston led by six.

Then Coach Lewis made a big mistake. Instead of continuing to run, he had the Cougars slow down and try to protect their lead.

NC State took advantage of the strategy. They forced a couple of turnovers and tied the game at 52.

With only seconds remaining, the Wolfpack looked to take the last shot. But the Cougars dug in and kept them away from the basket.

Finally, with less than five seconds remaining, NC

State guard Dereck Whittenberg put up a desperation jump shot from almost thirty feet away.

Down low, Hakeem watched the shot arc toward the basket. He saw that the ball was going to fall short. He knew he could easily catch it but was afraid the referees might call him for goaltending, giving the Wolfpack two points and the game.

The ball did fall short. But as Olajuwon reached for the rebound, NC State forward Lorenzo Charles snuck in, grabbed it, and dunked the ball just as time expired. Houston lost, 54–52!

The players were stunned. The defeat was one of the biggest upsets in NCAA tournament history.

Yet instead of dwelling on the disappointment, Hakeem immediately started looking ahead. Star forward Clyde Drexler left school for the NBA and was drafted in the first round. Several other players graduated. All of a sudden, Hakeem Olajuwon and forward Michael Young were the only two veterans on the team.

During practice before the 1983–84 season, Hakeem's role changed. Instead of his being the last option on offense, the Cougars' attack now featured him.

The offense usually began with one of the guards driving in and dishing the ball to Hakeem down low. If they were successful, Olajuwon was a threat to score on a jam, a layup, or a new shot he had developed, a short but deadly fadeaway jumper. But if his path to the basket was blocked, Hakeem had the good sense to find the open man and hit him with a pass. His offensive skills were beginning to catch up with his defensive prowess.

Once again, the Cougars stormed through the regular season, then charged through the NCAA tournament. For the third year running, they reached the Final Four. This time, Hakeem was determined to finish his season with a win.

They faced Virginia in the semifinals. Like NC State the year before, Virginia tried to take the Cougars out of their game by slowing down the tempo.

The strategy almost worked. Virginia forced the game into overtime, but Houston prevailed, 49–47.

The victory put the Cougars in the finals for the second year in a row. This time, they would play the Georgetown Hoyas.

Georgetown was led by center Patrick Ewing. Of

all the other players in college basketball, Olajuwon had more respect for Ewing than for anyone else.

The two young men had much in common. Like Hakeem, Patrick Ewing got a late start in basketball, never playing until he was thirteen years old. And also like Hakeem, Patrick was from a foreign country and had been raised in a different culture. Ewing was a native of Jamaica.

They even played a similar style, focusing on defense and shot blocking, although now, in his senior year, each player was beginning to be more assertive on offense. In years past, each had been expected to lead his team to an NCAA championship but, so far, had failed. They both would have only one more chance. Fans all over the country looked forward to the battle between the two best centers in college basketball.

But as sometimes happens when two players of equal skill meet, Ewing and Olajuwon canceled each other out. Each man played well but, because of the presence of the other, was unable to dominate.

After hitting seven straight shots and jumping out to a 14–6 lead, the Cougars got sloppy. Georgetown took advantage of that fact and went on a huge run, outscoring the Cougars 26–8. Both Olajuwon and Ewing got into foul trouble.

Down by ten at halftime, Cougar hopes faded when Olajuwon picked up his fourth foul just a few minutes into the second half. By the time he returned to the court, it was too late. Georgetown won, 84–75.

As the ecstatic Georgetown players celebrated on the court and cut down the nets, Hakeem sat on the bench with his head in his hands and cried. Although he had worked hard and come very far, he had lost.

There was still room for him to improve.

Chapter Seven:
1984-85

The Twin Towers

Immediately after the loss to Georgetown, Hakeem Olajuwon had to make a big decision, one almost as important as that which had led him from Africa to Houston nearly four years earlier. For although he had virtually completed his four years of undergraduate studies at Houston, he had played only three years of basketball. The NCAA ruled that if Hakeem wanted to, he could play one more season for the Cougars.

But Olajuwon's stellar performance over the past two seasons had brought him to the attention of the National Basketball Association. He was one of the most-sought-after players in college basketball. He knew that if he turned pro, he would probably be the first pick in the NBA draft. A professional career beckoned.

Star center for the University of Houston Cougars, Hakeem Olajuwon is head and shoulders above his opponents.

Wired for sound, Hakeem Olajuwon gets set for a shot before the 1983 Final Four.

Carrying over his soccer talents to the basketball court, Hakeem Olajuwon prepares for the 1984 Final Four.

Number 34 trades in his Cougar uniform to become a Rocket. He was the number one draft pick.

The Dream slams it home!

After beating the Orlando Magic for the NBA championship, Hakeem "the Dream" Olajuwon celebrates with teammate Clyde "the Glide" Drexler.

Hakeem is all smiles with his 1995 NBA Finals MVP award.

His rival since college, Patrick Ewing tries to stop Hakeem Olajuwon's bold move to the hoop.

A powerful two points!

Houston's superstar center blocks a shot against the Phoenix Suns.

Hakeem Olajuwon's Career Statistics

Year	G	FG%	3P%	FT%	RPG	APG	STL	BLK	PPG
1984-85	82	.538	—	.613	11.9	1.4	99	220	20.6
1985-86	68	.526	—	.645	11.5	2.0	134	231	23.5
1986-87	75	.508	.200	.702	11.4	2.9	140	254	23.4
1987-88	79	.514	.000	.695	12.1	2.1	162	214	22.8
1988-89	82	.508	.000	.696	13.5	1.8	213	282	24.8
1989-90	82	.501	.167	.713	14.0	2.9	174	376	24.3
1990-91	56	.508	.000	.769	13.8	2.3	121	221	21.2
1991-92	70	.502	.000	.766	12.1	2.2	127	304	21.6
1992-93	82	.529	.000	.779	13.0	3.5	150	342	26.1
1993-94	80	.528	.421	.716	11.9	3.6	128	297	27.3
1994-95	72	.517	.188	.756	10.8	3.5	133	242	27.8
1995-96	72	.514	.214	.724	10.9	3.6	113	207	26.9
1996-97	78	.510	.313	.787	9.2	3.0	117	173	23.2
Career	978	.516	.204	.716	12.0	2.7	1,811	3,363	24.2
All-Star	12	.409	1.000	.520	7.8	1.4	15	23	9.8
Playoff	115	.530	.286	.716	11.7	3.4	195	408	27.8

Hakeem Olajuwon's Career Highlights

1982: Member of NCAA Final Four team

1983: Named NCAA Final Four Most Outstanding Player
Member of NCAA Final Four team

1984: Member of NCAA Final Four team
Leads nation in shooting percentage and rebounding
Number one NBA draft pick

1985: Runner-up for Rookie of the Year

1986: Member of NBA championship finalist team

1989: Leads league in rebounding
First player in NBA history to post 200 blocked shots and
200 steals in one season

1990: Records a "quadruple double," the third in NBA history
Leads league in rebounding and blocked shots
Second player in NBA history to post more than 1,000
rebounds and 300 blocks in one season

1991: Leads league in blocked shots

1993: Leads league in blocked shots

1994: Winner of NBA MVP award
Member of NBA championship team
Winner of NBA Finals MVP award

1995: Member of NBA championship team
Winner of NBA Finals MVP award

1996: Selected as one of the "50 Greatest Players in NBA
History"
Ninth NBA player with career totals of at least 20,000
points and 10,000 rebounds
Olympic gold medal winner

Hakeem considered his choices carefully. If he played another season for the Cougars, there was a chance that he could lead the team to a national championship. But if he turned pro, there was a strong possibility that he would be selected by the Houston Rockets. If he were drafted by the Rockets, he would still be able to live in Houston, where he had made many friends and felt comfortable.

Since playing for the NBA championship in 1981, the Houston Rockets had fallen on hard times. Star center Moses Malone, Hakeem's friend, had left the team as a free agent and signed with Philadelphia. Two years later, the Rockets had the worst record in the Western Conference.

Houston and the Portland Trail Blazers each qualified for the first pick in the NBA draft. The NBA decided to flip a coin to determine which club would have the first chance to select Olajuwon.

Hakeem could not wait for the coin toss to make his decision. According to NBA rules, he had to make his decision to enter the draft before the toss.

Hakeem weighed his options. Over the past two seasons, as his offensive play had improved, the Cougars' opponents had started double- and triple-teaming him in an effort to prevent him from scoring. That made Hakeem feel as if he were surrounded by a group of annoying insects all game long. In the NBA, teams had to play man-to-man defense. He would have more room to move.

One other factor influenced his decision. Several key teammates were graduating. Hakeem wasn't sure if the team would be good enough to make it back to the Final Four no matter how well he played.

He decided to enter the NBA. But before the draft, he did something very special. He returned to Nigeria.

His parents and family were delighted to see him. Hakeem was happy to see them, too, but he was saddened by the conditions he saw in his country.

Since Hakeem had left, the strong Nigerian economy had faltered. The country looked as if it were falling apart.

His parents had not been able to avoid the economic troubles. Shortly after Hakeem arrived, he learned that his father was about to lose an apartment building he owned. He could not afford the mortgage payments.

Hakeem asked his father how much money he needed. His father said nearly ten thousand dollars.

Hakeem left the room and returned with an envelope. He handed it to his father.

"What's this?" Salam Olajuwon asked. Then he opened the envelope. It contained the money he needed, in traveler's checks. Even though Hakeem had not yet signed an NBA contract, he had enlisted the services of an agent, who had advanced him some money. The ability to help his parents, after they had done so much to help him, made Hakeem feel proud.

He stayed in Nigeria for three weeks. When he returned to America for the draft, he brought his parents and two of his younger brothers with him for a visit. They would all learn of Hakeem's future in the NBA together.

The Rockets won the coin toss. They selected Hakeem Olajuwon with the first pick of the draft. With the second pick, Portland picked center Sam Bowie of Kentucky. North Carolina's Michael Jordan was picked third by the Chicago Bulls.

Olajuwon was delighted. The year before, the Rockets had picked seven-foot-four-inch center

Ralph Sampson of Virginia, who had gone on to win the NBA's Rookie of the Year award. Now the team had two big men, and the Rockets planned to use them both. They were intrigued by the idea of having both centers on the court at the same time. So was Olajuwon. With Sampson around, he knew that he would have room to maneuver and play his game.

Rockets coach Bill Fitch knew just how to take advantage of his two talented big men. In training camp, he installed an offense that the press called the "Twin Towers," named after the two skyscrapers at the World Trade Center in New York. In the Twin Towers offense, Fitch had both Olajuwon and Sampson post up underneath the basket on either side of the free throw lane. The Rocket guards were supposed to penetrate and get the ball to either of the two centers.

If the defense collapsed down low, usually someone was open outside. If the defense played off the Twin Tower who got the ball, he was probably able to get off a good shot. Even if the shot missed, the other Tower was often there to put back the rebound for a basket.

Olajuwon and Sampson complemented each

other. Each played unselfishly. Hakeem usually stayed inside, grabbing rebounds and stuffing the ball back into the hoop, while Sampson, who had the moves of a much smaller man, occasionally stepped outside and shot the jumper.

The strategy worked well. The other NBA teams had a hard time matching up against the Twin Towers. On defense, each time an opponent drove down the lane, he was met by the Towers. Nearly every shot was challenged, and Olajuwon and Sampson scooped up virtually every rebound.

Although Hakeem played well, in many ways he was still learning the game. He was constantly trying out new strategies, particularly on defense, where he felt more comfortable. One move left his opponents particularly befuddled.

As the Rockets settled into their half-court defense, Hakeem Olajuwon would stay between his man and the basket, using his strength and size to keep the opposing player from getting too close to the hoop. Then, as the guards passed the ball back and forth on the perimeter looking for an opening, Hakeem would actually *duck down* and try to hide behind his man. Often, the man with the ball outside would look in, believe that the way to the basket was clear, and drive toward the hoop.

Surprise! As the player swooped toward the basket, Hakeem would pop out from behind the man he was guarding, leap up, and swat the ball from the man's hands just as he was preparing to shoot a layup! The driving player would be caught totally off guard. For the opposition, the Dream was a nightmare.

Competition within the NBA was strong when Olajuwon began his pro career. For several seasons, the Boston Celtics, Philadelphia 76ers, and Los Angeles Lakers had battled one another for the NBA championship. Each team was led by several superstars. The Celtics had Larry Bird, Kevin McHale, and Robert Parish. The 76ers were led by Julius "Doctor J" Erving and Moses Malone. Magic Johnson and legendary center Kareem Abdul-Jabbar paced the fast-breaking Lakers' attack.

But the Rockets weren't intimidated. In the preseason, they beat both the Celtics and the Lakers. At first, Hakeem found it hard to believe how strong and powerful the other centers in the league were. Compared with most of them, Hakeem Olajuwon, at six foot ten and 250 pounds, was actually *small*. Yet he soon discovered that by concentrating and using his quickness and jumping ability, he could hold his own against any center in the league.

The Rockets opened the 1984–85 season with eight straight wins. Soon, they were the big surprise of the season. With Olajuwon and Sampson leading the way, Houston's record improved by almost 20 games from the season before. With a record of 48–34, they finished second in the Midwest Division of the Western Conference, behind only the Denver Nuggets. Because of the way they had played against Boston, Philadelphia, and Los Angeles, some people thought the Rockets might challenge for the NBA title.

But first they had to make it through the playoffs. In the first round, they faced the Utah Jazz.

Utah featured the one player in the whole league who looked down on both Twin Towers. Gigantic center Mark Eaton was just a hair taller than Sampson and weighed nearly 300 pounds. He was widely considered the best defensive center in the league. Everyone looked forward to the matchup between Eaton and the Twin Towers.

It was no contest. Olajuwon and Sampson were

both much quicker than their opponent, and neither man had much difficulty scoring against him. But despite the performance of the Twin Towers, Houston's other team members didn't play very well. Houston guards John Lucas, Lewis Lloyd, and backup Lionel Hollins all struggled from the outside, making fewer than half their shots and scoring only two 3-point baskets the entire series. Meanwhile, paced by sharpshooting guard Darrell Griffith, the Jazz outplayed their counterparts. Houston lost to Utah in five games. The season was over.

For the third year in a row, Hakeem Olajuwon played for a team of championship caliber that had fallen short of its final goal. Despite Olajuwon's ending the season with a scoring average of better than 20 points per game and finishing second to Chicago Bulls guard Michael Jordan in the Rookie of the Year balloting, his presence had not been enough to lift the Rockets to the NBA title.

Although he was disappointed in the way the season ended, Hakeem Olajuwon knew he was on his way. Next year, he promised himself, he would try to complete his journey.

Chapter Eight:

1985–86

Finals Again

The 1985–86 Houston Rockets' lineup included most of the players who had been on the squad the previous year. The results, however, were very different.

Playing together for a second season helped everyone on the team. And Hakeem Olajuwon, in only his sixth year of basketball, was still getting better every day.

He spent the off-season in Houston. He bought his first home and spent the summer playing basketball at the Fonde Rec Center and working out in his gym at home.

Olajuwon used the pickup games at Fonde to work on his game. He knew that to reach his goal, he had to keep improving. And there was one aspect of his game in particular that needed work.

Although Hakeem was a dangerous offensive player under the basket, most NBA opponents didn't bother guarding him very closely when he was ten or twelve feet outside. In fact, they kept trying to push him away from the basket, where he wasn't an offensive threat. Then they could focus their defensive efforts on Ralph Sampson.

Olajuwon knew that he would have to make the defense pay for pushing him outside. All summer long, he worked on a quick, turnaround fadeaway jumper from the baseline. Although the fadeaway is a difficult shot to master, once perfected, it is hard to defend.

To get open, Hakeem would move out from the basket along the baseline. He'd set himself up about ten feet from the basket and call for the ball. If the defense overplayed him to one side or the other and left a lane to the basket open, he was still close enough to spin and go up for a dunk or a layup. But if they played him loose or the lane was closed, he used his new move.

Quick as lightning, he would pivot to face the basket and at the same time leap to take a jump shot. But instead of leaping straight up, Olajuwon would jump *away* from the basket. That's why the shot is called a fadeaway—because as the shooter jumps, he or she fades away from the basket.

Olajuwon spun and leapt so quickly that by the time the defense figured out he was going to shoot, it was too late to stop him. Because he was moving away from the basket, the shot was almost impossible to block. Olajuwon knew that if he could hit the shot consistently, it would open up the middle and make the Twin Towers even more difficult to stop.

The strategy worked. When the season began, the addition of the fadeaway jumper made Hakeem Olajuwon a much more dangerous offensive player.

The Rockets surged through the first two-thirds of the regular season. Hakeem was almost unstoppable, averaging nearly 25 points per game. The Rockets played as a team and were confident that they could beat anyone, even the Lakers and the Celtics.

Then catastrophe struck. The Rockets' star point guard, John Lucas, began playing erratically. With seventeen games left in the season, he tested positive for cocaine use and was suspended.

Although Lucas eventually overcame his addiction and turned his life around, becoming an NBA coach and drug abuse counselor, his late-season suspension threatened to ruin the Rockets' year.

But the team remained focused. They knew that with Lucas out of the lineup, every player on the team would have to step forward and play just a little better. They did just that and managed to capture the Midwest Division title with a record of 51–31. Yet most observers gave Houston little chance of advancing very far in the playoffs without Lucas running the offense.

The Rockets refused to fold. In the first round, they swept the Sacramento Kings in three games. Then they defeated the Denver Nuggets in a tough six-game series, earning the right to play the defending NBA champions, the Los Angeles Lakers, for the Western Conference championship.

The Lakers were more than their star player, Magic Johnson. James Worthy was super-quick and one of the best forwards in the league. And in the middle, the Lakers had Kareem Abdul-Jabbar.

Although he was thirty-eight years old, Abdul-Jabbar was still dangerous. At seven foot two, he had the size, strength, and experience to compete against any big man in basketball. Although he had started to slow down, he played smart. He was an excellent passer and his trademark sky-hook was unstoppable. If Abdul-Jabbar got the ball where he wanted it, the Lakers usually scored.

In the first game of the series, Magic keyed the Lakers' fast break while Abdul-Jabbar dominated inside. The Rockets lost, 119–107.

Houston was embarrassed. In game two the Rockets fought back.

Olajuwon and Sampson sparked the attack. Both men played aggressively from the start, particularly on defense. They knew that if they challenged every shot and fought for every rebound, the Lakers' fast break would have a hard time getting off the ground. They also went after Abdul-Jabbar, determined to make the cagey veteran work hard and tire out.

On defense they attacked the big man, forcing him to fight for position and pushing him away from the basket. On offense the Rockets knew that Abdul-Jabbar couldn't cover both Sampson and Olajuwon. And the Lakers really didn't have another player who could match up with either man. So when Abdul-Jabbar was guarding Sampson, the Rockets' offense turned to Olajuwon. Then, when Abdul-Jabbar switched over to cover Olajuwon, Sampson took over.

The Rockets won the next three games easily. With a victory in game five, they would reach the NBA finals.

But the Lakers refused to go down without a fight — literally. In a last-ditch effort to win, they tried to be the aggressors. Backup forwards Mitch Kupchak and Kurt Rambis were inserted into the lineup to bang around inside.

All game, Olajuwon fought off the swinging elbows and forearms of Kupchak. Then, in the fourth quarter with the score close, Kupchak caught Olajuwon with a savage elbow to the head.

Olajuwon had grown weary of the cheap shots and lost his cool. He threw a punch at Kupchak. Soon the two players were exchanging blows.

The referees stopped play, and members of both teams pulled the two men apart. Each was thrown out of the game.

Olajuwon immediately realized his mistake. Because he allowed Kupchak to goad him into a fight, the Lakers had come out on top. Although both players were ejected from the game, Kupchak was a second-stringer. Hakeem was a key member of the Rockets.

As Olajuwon watched on a TV in the locker room, his teammates dug in and refused to give up. With one second to play and the score tied, the Rockets had the ball.

Forward Rodney McCray inbounded the ball to Ralph Sampson. The big center used every inch of his height to outleap Abdul-Jabbar. Without landing, Sampson caught the ball and flicked it toward the basket.

The ball seemed to hang in the air for a moment before coming down.

Swish! The shot was good! The Rockets had beaten the Lakers! They were going to the NBA finals!

The team was ecstatic after the win, and Olajuwon was relieved to know that his mistake hadn't cost the game. But coach Bill Fitch warned the club not to get too excited. The Eastern Conference champions, the Boston Celtics, were even better than the Lakers. Fitch had once coached the Celtics and knew how well they could play.

The season before, the Celtics had lost to the

Lakers in the 1984–85 finals. In the off-season, the Celtics had improved their team dramatically with the addition of backup center Bill Walton. When healthy, the often-injured Walton was one of the best players in the game. All season long the Celtics had used him wisely, backing up star center Robert Parish or forward Kevin McHale and even using him in tandem with either man on occasion for their own version of the Twin Towers. They were the one team in the league that could match up against Olajuwon and Sampson.

With Larry Bird dominating the game with his outside shooting, passing, and rebounding, the Celtics appeared to be almost unbeatable. In two regular-season meetings, the Celtics had easily defeated the Rockets on their way to an NBA-best 67–15 record.

Just as Fitch had feared, the Rockets weren't focused for game one of the championship series. They lost 112–100, then were blown out in game two, 117–95.

Despite Houston's fighting back to win two of the next three, the Celtics easily won game six to capture the NBA title. Boston had matched up well with Houston down low, and without John Lucas, the

Rockets simply didn't have enough firepower from outside to make up the difference.

Hakeem Olajuwon played as well as he could in the playoffs, averaging more than 26 points per game, and led all players in scoring, rebounds, blocked shots, and field goal percentage.

Yet for all his efforts, he had still ended the season short of his goal. He began to wonder if he would ever be able to reach it, or whether he was a big man destined always to fall short.

Chapter Nine:

1986–92

Falling Apart

The Rockets began the 1986–87 season expecting once again to challenge for the NBA championship. But before the season was half over, disaster struck.

Ralph Sampson severely injured his knee. Although he returned to the lineup before the end of the season, he was never the same player again. For despite his height, Sampson had always built his game around quickness and agility. After the knee injury, he lost both. A potential Hall of Famer before the injury, Sampson became just another player afterward. One half of the Twin Towers had collapsed.

Olajuwon struggled to make up the difference. But only a few weeks after Sampson's injury, starting guards Mitchell Wiggins and Lewis Lloyd tested positive for drug use and were suspended from the league. The Rockets were officially grounded.

The team finished the season a disappointing 42–40, third in the Midwest Division. Although they defeated the Portland Trail Blazers in the first round of the playoffs, in the second round the Seattle SuperSonics won in six games, ending Houston's dismal season once and for all.

Over the next few years, the Rockets appeared to be running in place. New coach Don Chaney replaced Bill Fitch, but the change had little impact. Although Houston remained competitive with a record that hovered just above .500, the Rockets failed to recover from the disastrous 1986–87 season. Ralph Sampson was traded away. Even though John Lucas, Lewis Lloyd, and Mitchell Wiggins all eventually returned to Houston's lineup, the chemistry of the team had been destroyed.

Each of the next four seasons, the Rockets qualified for the playoffs but went out quietly in the first round, twice to Magic Johnson's Los Angeles Lakers. There was no secret to stopping the Rockets. On offense and defense, the Rockets began and ended with Hakeem Olajuwon.

When the Rockets had the ball, the opposition had one goal — keep it away from Olajuwon. The other Rockets weren't much of a threat to score, so unless Olajuwon exploded for 30 or 40 points, Houston had a hard time making enough baskets to win.

It was no different on defense. The opposition usually had its biggest and toughest player try to occupy Olajuwon, pushing him away from the basket and making him fight through screens. Houston's opponents knew that if they ran their offense away from Hakeem, they could score easily.

Game after game, the newspaper story line was often the same: Olajuwon played well, but the Rockets lost.

In both the 1988–89 and 1989–90 seasons, Olajuwon led the NBA in rebounding, and he led the league in blocked shots in 1989–90 and 1990–91. In 1988–89, he also became the first player in NBA history ever to finish in the top ten in scoring, rebounding, steals, and blocks for two consecutive seasons.

Whenever a player reaches double figures — ten or more — in three of the four major offensive categories (points, rebounds, blocks, and assists), it is called a triple-double. A player who gets a triple-double has played a well-rounded game. While not rare, triple-doubles don't happen in every game.

Much rarer is a quadruple-double, meaning the player has reached double figures in all four offensive categories. That has happened only three times in NBA history. On March 29, 1990, in a game against the Milwaukee Bucks, Hakeem Olajuwon turned in one of the best individual performances in NBA history. Olajuwon had a quadruple-double!

Olajuwon did everything that day, yet he didn't really appear to stand out. His contributions all came in the context of Houston's team play. On offense, he scored a quiet 18 points, taking the ball to the hoop when he had an opening. But he passed off when he didn't and so collected 11 assists. He grabbed only a few more rebounds than usual, for a total of 16 for the game, but he really excelled at blocking shots. Almost every time a Milwaukee player charged toward the basket, there was Olajuwon. Eleven different times he swatted the ball away from the hoop.

Hakeem tried not to get frustrated and worked to continue improving his game. As the focus of the Houston attack, Olajuwon now touched the ball on nearly every possession. He became an increasingly adept ball handler and started to feel confident about putting the ball on the floor. He developed the ability to go one-on-one with a defender.

That made it hard for most big men in the NBA to defend him. Olajuwon was simply too quick for most centers in the league. Yet if they tried to cover him with a forward, Olajuwon would use his superior strength and height down low.

The Rockets liked to get him the ball low along the baseline. Then, with his back to the basket, he would hold the ball in front, faking passes back outside to his guards or to the forwards cutting to the hoop. All the time, Olajuwon would feel his defender on his back, sensing exactly how he was being defended.

Then, as soon as he felt the defender commit to a certain strategy, Olajuwon went into action. If the defender tried to get in front of Hakeem to block a pass or knock the ball from his hands, *Swwoosh!* Hakeem would duck and spin around him, then go up for a slam dunk. And if Hakeem felt the defender pushing him away from the basket, he would hold his ground for a moment, then spin out for a fade-away. But sometimes neither of those two options was available. So Hakeem developed a deadly jump hook from short range and the uncanny ability to pass the ball to the open man.

But no matter how well Olajuwon played, the Rockets failed to improve. Some observers even blamed Olajuwon for the team's poor performance, believing that he had become a selfish player. They didn't realize that he was shooting so much because the Rockets had so few other weapons.

The criticism and the constant losing affected Hakeem. He had always been happy, but now he often became discouraged. For just as the Rockets appeared to be running in place, so did Hakeem Olajuwon. He broke up with his longtime girlfriend and felt empty inside. No matter how much he scored or how much money he made, he was not happy.

Then one day in Houston, after practice, a man approached him and asked, "Are you a Muslim?" Olajuwon said that he was. The two men began talking about the religion, and Hakeem admitted that he had never taken the religion as seriously as he should have.

The man told him there was an Islamic mosque, or

church, in Houston and invited Hakeem to visit and pray. In the Islamic religion, believers pray at special times each day, either in private or at the mosque with others.

Olajuwon agreed to accompany the man; as soon as he entered the mosque and began praying, he realized what had been missing in his life. Since coming to America, he had slowly lost sight of his heritage and his roots. By returning to the Islamic religion, he was able to recapture his old self and gain perspective on life. He learned to look beyond his day-to-day struggles and focus on larger goals. He immediately felt more comfortable in his life.

But there was more to being a Muslim than praying. Muslims are prohibited from drinking alcohol, earning interest on money, or eating pork. During the month of Ramadan, a special religious holiday, Muslims are required to fast from dawn until dusk. They cannot even drink a sip of water.

Hakeem Olajuwon committed himself to observing all Islamic customs. During Ramadan, which begins in mid-April and continues through mid-May, he had to be extra careful and make certain he ate and drank enough at night so he would remain strong enough to play. In his private life, he stopped hanging out with anyone who indulged in bad behavior. On the court, he stopped focusing so much on winning and losing. Instead, he learned to play simply for the joy of it, just as he had when he first started playing the game in Africa. He recaptured the glee he had felt the first time he dunked the basketball. If the Rockets won, he was pleased, but even if they lost, as long as he played with joy and in the proper spirit, he was satisfied.

As he wrote in his autobiography, he decided that he wanted "to be remembered as a great person; not the greatest player in the world but a person who was honest and gracious and honorable." For if he could succeed as a person, he knew he would succeed as a player. As he later told an interviewer, he realized that "basketball is just a little aspect of my life. I enjoy the game because it's fun. But it is just a game."

Of course, what Olajuwon soon discovered was that playing with joy led to playing better and winning more often. He felt invigorated, and his play improved dramatically. He had never felt so energetic or full of life.

In the off-season, he began working with a trainer

and practicing hard to improve his game. He realized that the moves he had developed to use underneath the basket could work from the outside as well and could force the defense to come out after him, opening up the inside. To his other moves he added a simple jump shot that he could take off the dribble and shoot from twenty feet. He was becoming a complete player.

But few people apart from the opposition realized it. The Rockets had been playing .500 basketball for so many years that when the best players in the league were discussed, Hakeem's name came up almost as an afterthought. He had the stats but not the recognition.

That experience is common among many great athletes. Until a player wins a championship, he is not respected by others. Even Michael Jordan, probably the best basketball player ever, was criticized for being selfish until he led the Bulls to an NBA championship. Olajuwon was in a similar position.

In 1990, the Rockets finally began to rebuild, adding point guard Kenny Smith to stabilize the backcourt. Power forward Otis Thorpe emerged to complement Olajuwon down low. Houston started the 1990–91 season strong, but in January Olajuwon was hit in the face by the elbow of an opposing player and fractured his eye socket. Although he missed only eight weeks of the season, the Rockets still went out of the playoffs in the first round.

The team failed to improve in the 1991–92 season, even though Olajuwon was playing better than ever. In an effort to shake things up, near the end of the season the Rockets fired coach Don Chaney and replaced him with former Rocket Rudy Tomjanovich.

Tomjanovich was the perfect man for the position. Although the team missed the playoffs, as soon as the season ended, Tomjanovich started putting back together what had fallen apart.

Chapter Ten:
1992-94

A Final Chance

Hakeem Olajuwon respected his new coach. Rudy Tomjanovich had been an NBA star and was well known for being tough but fair.

The respect was mutual. Tomjanovich believed that Olajuwon was one of the most talented players in the game. He installed an offense very similar to the old Twin Towers concept that had once been so successful. Only now there was just one Tower — Hakeem.

The Rockets also added several talented players that gave them more depth. Rookie forward Robert Horry filled a void at small forward, and Carl Herrera provided a much-needed power forward off the bench.

It took the first half of the 1992–93 season for the Rockets to adapt to the new offense. At the All-Star break, they were in third place. Then they started clicking.

Olajuwon thrived under Coach Tomjanovich. His added responsibility on offense increased his confidence in his game, and his talented teammates gave him all the support he needed.

Hakeem Olajuwon was a total player. With the jumper in his repertoire and the ability to dribble and handle the basketball as well as any big man in the game, he was a threat from any spot on the court. And despite his increased focus on offense, he remained a dominant defensive force.

In many minds, he was the best player in the NBA, or at least second only to Michael Jordan. He was named to the All-NBA first team for the fourth time, beating out other star centers like Patrick Ewing, Shaquille O'Neal, David Robinson, and Alonzo Mourning and was selected as the NBA Defensive Player of the Year. He averaged a career-high 26.1 points per game, fourth-best in the league, and blocked more than four shots per game.

Late in the season, the Rockets reeled off 15 straight victories to win the Midwest Division with a 55–27 record. For the first time in years, the team entered the playoffs feeling like it could win.

And Houston did in the first round, dumping the Los Angeles Clippers. Then, in the second round, they ran into the Seattle SuperSonics.

The two teams fought a tough seven-game battle, but Seattle edged out Houston in the final game. It was "wait until next year" for the Rockets again. But instead of dwelling on the past, they were looking forward with eager anticipation of what was to come. Olajuwon knew the team was on the right track.

At the end of the season, he also took care of some important unfinished business. He decided to become an American citizen.

Hakeem had been considering becoming a citizen for several years. He felt at home in America and knew he would spend the rest of his life in the United States. His brothers now lived in the United States, and his parents were frequent visitors. He remained proud of his Nigerian heritage but was troubled by the direction his country had been going. So on April 2, 1993, Hakeem Olajuwon became an American citizen.

Houston and the rest of the NBA got a break just before the beginning of the 1993–94 season.

Michael Jordan, fresh from leading the Bulls to three consecutive NBA championships, shocked the basketball world by announcing his retirement to play professional baseball. His absence left the NBA title up for grabs.

No one went after it harder than Hakeem Olajuwon. In 1993–94, he followed the best season of his career with an even better one.

With Hakeem leading the way, the Rockets jumped out to the quickest start in NBA history, winning their first fifteen games and sending a message to the rest of the league that the Rockets were championship caliber.

When the team stumbled a bit at mid-season, Olajuwon refused to give up. He paced them on a late-season charge that once again led to the Midwest Division title. The league recognized his achievement by naming him the NBA's Most Valuable Player.

Houston began the playoffs by quickly dispatching the Portland Trail Blazers. Then the Rockets met the Phoenix Suns in round two.

The team might have been looking past the Suns because the Seattle SuperSonics, winners of a league-best 63 games, had been upset in the first round of the playoffs, leaving the Rockets with the best record of any team still playing. They knew the title was theirs for the taking. The series opened with two games in Houston, and the Rockets felt as if they were poised for a sweep.

But the Suns had other ideas. After falling behind by 18 points in game one, Phoenix rallied to win, 91–87. Then in game two, the Rockets appeared to hit their stride. With only ten minutes remaining, they led by 20. Houston thought the game was over.

They forgot to tell the Suns. Phoenix outscored the Rockets 24–4 over the remainder of the quarter to force the game into overtime. Then they went on to win.

The Rockets were stunned. Coach Tomjanovich called a team meeting in Phoenix the next day.

Hakeem Olajuwon proved that he was the most valuable player in the league both on and off the court. He took command.

Speaking softly but strongly, he told Tomjanovich and the entire team what they had to do to win. He blamed their recent collapse on the fatigue of the Houston starters and admonished his coach to use his entire roster. Tomjanovich and Olajuwon had such respect for each other that the coach listened to the advice of his star player.

Then Hakeem addressed his teammates. He knew everyone was feeling tense after losing the first two games at home.

"Everybody says the pressure is on us now," he said, "but the pressure is really on them. Now everybody expects them to win.

"If we win tonight," he added, "they will choke."

Olajuwon's words fired up his teammates. They survived an early charge that put the Suns up by 14 points in the first quarter to come to within nine by halftime. Then, as the Rockets drew closer in the second half, the Suns started to feel the pressure, just as Olajuwon had predicted. The Rockets took over and won, 118–102.

Keyed by the play of the Houston bench, the Rockets stormed back to take the series from the Suns and move on to the third round of the playoffs. They maintained their momentum and dumped the Utah Jazz in five games. With sheer determination and hard work, they had earned the right to play for the NBA championship.

Their opponents were the New York Knicker-bockers.

The two teams were very similar. Both played tough, physical defense, and on offense, each team shot a lot of three-pointers. But the greatest similarity was in the middle. Both teams had a big man: Olajuwon of the Rockets, and Patrick Ewing of the New York Knicks.

Olajuwon and Ewing, old college rivals, still had the utmost respect for each other. Their pro careers had continued to parallel each other. While both were the same tough rebounders and defensive intimidators they had been in the NCAA, each had blossomed into an offensive star in the NBA. Each man was the heart of his team's offense. As Olajuwon once said of Ewing, "He is a warrior, who comes to play. I did not think he was better than I was, but I also didn't think I was better than Patrick." Basketball fans all over the country looked forward to the matchup between Olajuwon and Ewing.

The series opened in Houston, and New York set the tone in the first game. The Knicks' physical, swarming defense stopped the Rockets' fast break.

But Houston responded in kind and won the defensive struggle, 85–78. After the game, Coach Tomjanovich announced to the team, "It's a war."

Olajuwon was in the center of the battle. Unlike most teams, the Knicks refused to double-team him when he had the ball. Instead, they played him man-to-man. But rather than using a single player, like Patrick Ewing, to try to contain Hakeem, they substituted often and had a variety of players cover him. By doing so, they hoped Olajuwon would grow weary.

The strategy worked — sort of. All through the series, Olajuwon played well in bursts. Then the Knicks would change defenders and shut him down.

But at the same time, Olajuwon was able to keep Ewing in check. Although both men played well at times, neither was able to get the upper hand. Just as had happened when the two players faced each other in the Final Four, they nearly canceled each other out.

In the end, it appeared that the series would be determined from the outside. The team that shot best from long range would win.

Entering game six, that team looked to be the Knicks. They had come back from their first-game loss to win three of the next four, including two of the three games played in New York. Knick guards John Starks and Derek Harper were outshooting their counterparts. Returning to Houston for game six, the Knicks needed only one win to capture the championship.

The two teams went after each other like heavyweight boxers throwing their best punches. But neither team would fall.

Late in the fourth quarter, the Rockets led 84–82. It was New York's ball. John Starks came off a screen set by Patrick Ewing and got the pass.

Usually when Starks got the ball off a screen, he put it in the air. His sharpshooting thus far had kept New York in the game. But this time Starks tried to do something different. Instead of shooting, he tried to shovel a pass back to Ewing down low. He figured the pass would surprise the Rockets.

Wrong! As Hakeem Olajuwon commented after the game, "There are no surprises now." In his long career, he had seen almost everything. As Starks made his move, Olajuwon pushed around Ewing and got his hand on the ball. Houston recovered the ball and went ahead 86–82.

But New York scored another basket, then got the ball back. With only two seconds left to play the Knicks prepared to inbound from under their own basket.

Once again, the Knicks looked for John Starks. He wove his way through the Houston defense, then came off another screen set by Patrick Ewing. As soon as Starks popped free, Knick forward Anthony Mason inbounded the ball to him just beyond the three-point line.

Olajuwon followed the play carefully. When Starks came off the screen, he pushed around Ewing. If Starks came back with a pass to Ewing, Olajuwon wanted to be in position to pick it off.

But this time Starks had his mind on shooting. A three-pointer, his specialty, would win the game, and the championship for New York.

As Starks squared himself to face the basket, the clock clicked down to one second. Olajuwon saw that Starks was going to shoot and made a decision. He would go for the block.

But Starks was too far away for Olajuwon to knock the ball from his hands. The big man's only chance was to leap up and try to block the ball after it left

Starks's hands. There was no margin for error. If he missed, and the shot went in, he would finish second best again.

Starks jumped, raising the ball above his head. Olajuwon took one quick step and took off.

He slipped! As Olajuwon jumped, he was totally out of control.

Yet he still reached out for the spot in the air he thought the ball would be.

Starks released the ball. Olajuwon's hand met it spinning through space. The ball deflected away from the basket just as the buzzer sounded.

86–84, the Rockets won!

Though they still had to play game seven, New York simply couldn't recover. In the final game of the series, John Starks made only 2 of 18 shots, while Olajuwon controlled the middle and tossed in a game-high 25 points. The Rockets won, 90–84, to win the NBA championship.

The ball was in Olajuwon's hands as the final buzzer sounded and the crowd poured from the stands onto the court of the Summit. Olajuwon said a quick prayer and dashed from the court to the locker room, where he was swarmed by the media. Before leaving the arena, he found Patrick Ewing and embraced him, saying, "You did all you could. Don't lose hope."

At a news conference the next day, Olajuwon accepted the NBA Finals MVP award, becoming the first player ever to win the league MVP, the Defensive Player of the Year, and the NBA Finals MVP award in the same season. It had been a long, long journey, but he had finally made it to the top.

Two days later, he was back on the court in Houston, playing a pickup game. After all, basketball was just a game Hakeem Olajuwon played for fun.

Chapter Eleven:
1994–95

Repeat After Me

Only a handful of teams in the history of the NBA have ever been able to win back-to-back NBA championships. Entering the 1994–95 season, the Michael Jordan–led Chicago Bulls, the Boston Celtics, the Detroit Pistons, and the Minneapolis and Los Angeles Lakers had won consecutive titles. Now, the Rockets had a chance to repeat.

They got off to a good start, winning their first nine games. But then the team got overconfident. All of a sudden they stopped playing together. By mid-season, Houston was in danger of not even qualifying for the playoffs.

The Rockets decided that they had to do something. The Portland Trail Blazers were in a similar position, also needing to make a change to shake the team up. The Trail Blazers believed that All-Star guard/forward Clyde Drexler, Hakeem Olajuwon's former teammate at the University of Houston and a twelve-year NBA veteran, was starting to slow down. They let other teams in the league know that he was available in a trade.

One day after practice, Coach Tomjanovich asked Olajuwon how he would feel playing with his old teammate again. Hakeem just looked at the coach, stunned.

Olajuwon thought Drexler might be the solution to Houston's troubles. For apart from Olajuwon, the Rockets were primarily a team of role players. In order to win, everyone had to do his job and they all had to play together as a team. Otherwise, they simply weren't very good.

But he couldn't believe that Portland would ever trade Drexler. As far as Olajuwon was concerned, his friend was still one of the best players in the NBA. He told Tomjanovich to go for it.

Hakeem felt that Drexler would add a whole new dimension to the club. Not only was Clyde Drexler a team player, he was also one of the best one-on-one players in the game. In the past when things got tough, the Rockets had always turned to Olajuwon.

He was the only player they had who could make things happen. With Drexler on the court with him, Hakeem knew the Rockets would have another option. The opposition would have to worry about both men.

Several days later, in mid-February, the Rockets traded forward Otis Thorpe for Drexler and forward Tracy Murray. Although Olajuwon hated to lose Thorpe, a valuable teammate, Portland wouldn't make the trade unless it included Thorpe. Olajuwon believed the move was for the good of the team.

At first, the deal seemed to backfire. The Rockets expected Carl Herrera to step into Thorpe's place at power forward, but he got hurt. Then they tried to make a trade, but in the NBA each team has to operate within a salary cap, a specific amount of money a team is allowed to spend on players. There was no way under the cap for the Rockets to acquire another premium player.

The deal caused other problems, too. Drexler's presence cut into the playing time of the Rockets guards, a situation that displeased several players and threatened to tear the team apart. Then things got worse.

Olajuwon started feeling run-down. He had recently completed his observance of Ramadan, and thought his fatigue might be related to that.

Then team doctors tested his blood and discovered that he was suffering from anemia, an iron deficiency that results in fatigue. They concluded that it wasn't Ramadan that had caused the problem but rather the use of anti-inflammatory medication Olajuwon had been taking for a series of small injuries. Another Houston player, Vernon Maxwell, then came down with the same affliction.

Both players had to rest for a few weeks and take iron supplements to recover. Meanwhile, the team floundered.

Fortunately for Houston, however, several other teams hit bad streaks right at the end of the season. The Rockets made the playoffs with a 47–35 record, but they were seeded sixth in the Western Conference. In the first round, they would have to face Utah, winners of 60 games in the regular season. Moreover, even if they got past the Jazz, the Rockets would have to play most of their playoff games on the road, where it is always more difficult to win. The road back to the NBA championship was the toughest imaginable.

No one expected the Rockets to repeat as champions, particularly after their first playoff game. Utah won by two and after the game Rocket guard Vernon Maxwell, upset over decreased playing time because of Drexler, didn't show up for practice and was suspended. The Rockets' season looked to be over.

Then Olajuwon and Drexler came back to life. The two veterans knew how to play in crunch time.

Utah didn't give in, but Drexler and Olajuwon took over the series. Their stellar performance allowed other players, like guard Kenny Smith, to get open and make three-point shots. Not even the loss of forward Carl Herrera to a separated shoulder could stop the Rockets. They beat Utah in five games.

That simply earned the team the right to play the powerful Phoenix Suns, who had finished the season with the third-best record in the league and started the postseason by sweeping Portland. They were a powerful, versatile team, built around forward Charles Barkley and guard Kevin Johnson.

The Suns won the first two games in Phoenix in blowouts, 130–108 and 118–94. Back in Houston, the Rockets won game three but blew a late lead in game four to fall behind in the series three games to one. One more loss would end their season. In order to continue, the Rockets had to win three in a row.

In Phoenix for game five, Olajuwon rallied his teammates as the Rockets waited to go onto the floor. He wanted to make sure his teammates played one game at time and remained focused. "This is the championship game," he said. "Let's go out and surprise them."

They did, playing well for most of the game. But with seconds left, Houston trailed by two.

Hakeem Olajuwon had the ball. With five fouls, he was afraid to drive to the basket, where he might get called for charging. Instead, he demonstrated why some observers considered him the most complete player in the game.

Instead of driving, he circled the lane with his back to the basket as Sun center Danny Schayes pushed him away. Then he suddenly spun, stepped back, and launched a fadeaway. Schayes couldn't touch it.

Swish! The shot tied the game! Sparked by their

center's game-saving bucket, the Rockets dug in, played tough, and won in overtime, 103–97.

They followed with a victory in game six, 116–103, too, setting up a game-seven showdown in Phoenix. The Suns were on the ropes. They lost a close game. The Rockets advanced to the next round, the conference championship.

The San Antonio Spurs had finished the regular season with the best record in the league. So far, they had marched through the playoffs like they were the best team. Center David Robinson, the league MVP, had been remarkable all year long. In the regular season, the Spurs had defeated Houston in five of six games. Once again, no one gave the Rockets a chance.

No one, that is, except Hakeem Olajuwon and his teammates. Olajuwon respected Robinson and the Spurs, but he did not fear them. He was confident that if he played his game, the Rockets would win.

He did even more than that. He responded with the best play of his career.

In game one he scored 27 points and hit Robert Horry with a spectacular pass that Horry converted for the winning basket in a 94–93 victory. The win gave the team momentum entering game two, and they won again, 106–96. The Rockets returned to Houston up two games to none.

But the Spurs refused to give in and won the next two games to even up the series. Now the pressure was on Houston.

Olajuwon took control, scoring 42 points as the Rockets routed San Antonio 111–90. The Rockets were one game away from the finals.

Olajuwon made sure there was no letdown. In a head-to-head matchup against the league MVP in the most important game of the year, he left everyone open-mouthed with wonder.

He was unstoppable, spinning in for slams, spinning back for fadeaways, tossing in jump hooks, and even throwing in a few twenty-foot jumpers for good measure. He scored 39 points, hauled down 17 rebounds, and shut down Robinson completely. The Spurs center made only 6 of 19 shots and gathered only 10 rebounds. The Rockets won, 100–95.

After the game, David Robinson shook his head in awe of Olajuwon, acknowledging that he had been completely outplayed. "I've never felt this way before," he said. "For the first time in my life, I let my teammates down."

The humble Olajuwon gave Robinson credit for his performance. "When you play a center of David's caliber, that makes it more competitive." Robinson, added Olajuwon, had forced him to perform at his highest level.

Houston faced one final challenge. Keyed by the play of their gigantic center, Shaquille O'Neal, and point guard Penny Hardaway, the Orlando Magic had won the Eastern Conference championship, even defeating the Chicago Bulls, who played well after Michael Jordan returned to basketball late in the season. In many eyes, the Magic, with Shaq and Penny, were the team of the future.

It certainly looked that way in the first quarter of game one. The Magic jumped out to a 30–15 lead. At halftime, they still led by 11 as O'Neal's aggressive play put Olajuwon into foul trouble.

But Rocket guard Kenny Smith got hot in the second half, draining three-pointers. Then, with ten seconds left to play, the Magic lost a chance to go ahead by seven when Magic guard Nick Anderson missed four straight foul shots. Smith then hit another three-pointer to send the game into overtime.

With only five seconds left to play in overtime and the score knotted, Clyde Drexler drove to the basket. O'Neal left Olajuwon and went for the block.

He missed but forced Drexler to alter his shot. The ball banged off the rim toward Olajuwon.

Alone under the basket, the Rockets' big man simply jumped up and tapped the ball into the basket. The Rockets won!

The tough loss broke Orlando's spirit. Houston won game two in a rout, 117–106, then followed with another big win in game three. One more victory would deliver a second consecutive championship to Houston.

In the fourth game, the Magic dug in, leading by four at halftime. At the end of the third quarter, Houston led by one. Both teams were in a position to win.

But the Rockets knew how to play and win an NBA final. With victory in sight, they would not be denied.

Drexler and Olajuwon took over down the stretch, hitting the big shots, passing to the open man, and hauling down key rebounds. With less than fifteen seconds remaining, the Rockets led by nine, 110–101.

They worked the ball around outside, trying to wait out the clock. Olajuwon even raced to help out.

He got the ball. A decade before, the notion of having Hakeem Olajuwon handle the ball outside would have been unthinkable. Now, there was no player on the entire team who was better with the basketball.

Hakeem turned to face the basket. The clock was running down. He squared, jumped, and shot.

The ball arced high above the basket, then dropped. The referee threw up his hands. A three-pointer for Olajuwon!

Time expired a few seconds later. The Rockets had swept the Magic in four games. For the second year in a row, they were champions!

By a unanimous vote, Olajuwon was named the Most Valuable Player of the championship series. In sixteen of Houston's twenty-two playoff games, Olajuwon had scored 30 or more points. Against the Magic, he had completely dominated Shaquille O'Neal, averaging 33 points, 11 rebounds, 5 assists, and 2 blocks per game. On its way to the championship, Houston, the lowest seed ever to win the title, had won a remarkable nine games on the road, a playoff best.

"No team has done what this team has done," announced Coach Tomjanovich after the game. "I want to tell the nonbelievers something," he said in reference to those who had given the Rockets no chance to repeat. "Don't ever underestimate the heart of a champion."

Then he looked at Hakeem Olajuwon, who stood nearby with a weary smile on his face. Everyone knew who Tomjanovich was referring to.

At the ceremony awarding the team the championship trophy, NBA Commissioner David Stern looked over at Hakeem and beamed, "I'm not allowed to cheer, but even I have become a Hakeem Olajuwon fan."

Millions of basketball fans agreed.

Chapter Twelve:
1995–96

The Dream Continues

By the end of the 1994–95 season, Hakeem Olajuwon had established himself as one of the greatest players in the history of the NBA. His career totals for points and rebounds ranked him among the game's elite players. By the end of the 1995–96 season, he became only the ninth player in the history of the league to amass more than 20,000 points and 10,000 rebounds; Olajuwon also became the all-time NBA leader in blocked shots, with more than 3,000 to his credit.

But despite his personal achievements, Olajuwon was more concerned about the performance of the Rockets. The team was riddled with injuries all year long, yet still limped to a 48–34 record. It was the twelfth year in a row that the Olajuwon-led squad finished with a record of .500 or better.

In the playoffs, the Rockets faced the Los Angeles Lakers, a tough squad made even tougher by the return of Magic Johnson. But Houston prevailed. After defeating the Lakers, the Rockets met their old nemesis, the Seattle SuperSonics.

Seattle had won the previous nine meetings against Houston. Once again, few people gave the Rockets much of a chance.

This time, they were right. Paced by forward Sean Kemp, the Sonics swept the first three games. The Rockets refused to give in, however, and fought back from a 20-point fourth-quarter deficit to force an overtime before losing the fourth game. For the first time in three seasons, the Rockets watched the remainder of the playoffs at home.

But Olajuwon's season wasn't over. In 1992, he had watched with envy as the U.S. Olympic men's basketball team, dubbed the Dream Team, swept its way to a gold medal. The squad was mostly NBA players, including Michael Jordan and Larry Bird. Because he was not yet a U.S. citizen, Olajuwon hadn't been eligible to play for the United States. And because of his feelings about the current Nigerian government, he chose not to play for his native country.

All that had changed by 1996. As a U.S. citizen, Hakeem Olajuwon was eligible for the team. To no one's surprise, he was an easy selection. After all, how could there be another Dream Team without the Dream himself?

Although the 1996 Dream Team didn't have quite as easy a time as its 1992 counterparts, it still won the gold medal handily, defeating Yugoslavia, 95–69, in the final game.

True to form, Olajuwon used the Olympics as an opportunity to become friends with athletes from around the world as well as with so many of the players he did battle against during the regular season. He played relatively little, allowing teammates David Robinson and Shaquille O'Neal to log the majority of the available minutes at center. As the team's elder statesman, Olajuwon saw his role as making certain that everyone played together as a team.

Now, as he enters the twilight of what will certainly be a Hall of Fame career, Olajuwon has begun to look beyond basketball. Before the 1996–97 season, he married Dalia Asafi in a traditional Muslim ceremony. While he continues to perform at the peak of his profession, Olajuwon remains concerned with more than basketball. His dreams extend far beyond the court. For as he told an interviewer, "You're only a true professional if you carry yourself right at all times — off the floor, on the floor, every night, every game.

"When people talk about my popularity as a basketball player," he added later, "they don't know that I'm not in competition with anybody, because I am comfortable with myself. All the boundaries in the world are set by men. But you don't have to look at boundaries when you are looking at a man. The question is: What do you stand for? Are you a follower, or are you a leader?"

Hakeem Olajuwon is unquestionably a leader, one of the most thoughtful and talented players ever to perform in the NBA. He expects nothing less than the best from himself. After all, in Olajuwon's native language, the name *Hakeem* means "always on top." His journey continues.

END

Read them all!

All available in paperback from Little, Brown and Company

Matt Christopher